BLOOMINGTON PUBLIC LIBRARY
W9-AYV-931

GUS and GRANDPA and Show-and-Tell

Claudia Mills ★ Pictures by Catherine Stock

Farrar, Straus and Giroux
New York

For Christopher and Gregory
—C.M.

For Harry and Benjamin
—C.S.

Distributed in Canada by Douglas & McIntyre Ltd.
Color separations by Berryville Graphics/All Systems Color
Printed in the United States of America
First edition, 2000
1 3 5 7 9 10 8 6 4 2

Library of Congress Cataloging-in-Publication Data
Mills, Claudia.
Gus and Grandpa and show-and-tell / Claudia Mills ; pictures by Catherine Stock. — 1st ed.
p. cm.
Summary: Gus despairs of coming up with something interesting and impressive for his second-grade class's show-and-tell, until he gets a great idea while visiting Grandpa.
ISBN 0-374-32819-6
[1. Show-and-tell presentations—Fiction. 2. Schools—Fiction. 3. Grandfathers—Fiction.] I. Stock, Catherine, ill. II. Title.
PZ7.M63963Gudg 2000
[E]—dc21 99-21166

Contents

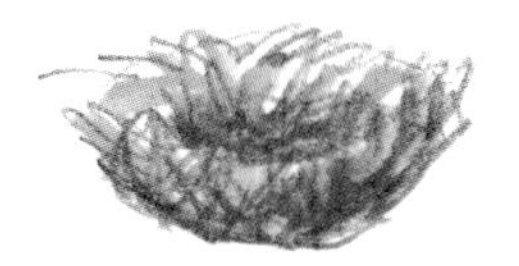

CIRCUS

Nothing to Show, Nothing to Tell

Gus liked everything
about second grade,
except for show-and-tell.
In first grade,
you could bring anything you liked
for show-and-tell.
Gus had brought cool stuff:
baseball cards
and a plastic rattlesnake
and the super-duper flashlight
Grandpa had given him for Christmas.

In second grade,
Mrs. Hall sent home a list of topics
for show-and-tell.
Gus could never think of cool stuff
to bring anymore.

This week the topic was
natural habitats.
"Do we have any natural habitats
that I can take
for show-and-tell?"
Gus asked his parents.

"How about a bird's nest?"
his dad said.
But they couldn't find any.

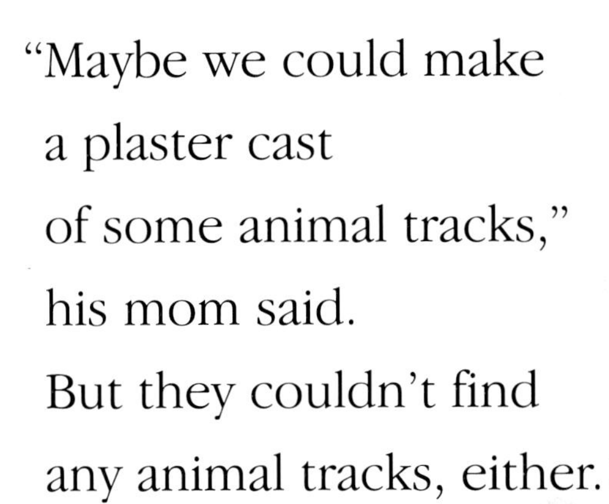

"Maybe we could make
a plaster cast
of some animal tracks,"
his mom said.
But they couldn't find
any animal tracks, either.

Gus ended up bringing
a dumb picture of a beaver lodge
cut out from a magazine.

Melissa Vogel brought
a bird's nest.
Alex Kahn brought
a plaster cast of animal tracks.

Ryan Mason brought
a huge model of a beaver lodge,
which he had made,
and two long books about beavers,
which he had read all by himself,
and a real beaver's tail.

Gus was starting to hate
show-and-tell.
Compared to Ryan Mason,
he had nothing to show;
he had nothing to tell.

Solids, Liquids, and Gases

The next week,
Gus told his parents,
"I need a solid,
a liquid, or a gas
for show-and-tell."

"That should be easy,"
Gus's father said.
"Everything is a solid,
a liquid, or a gas.
You can take anything."

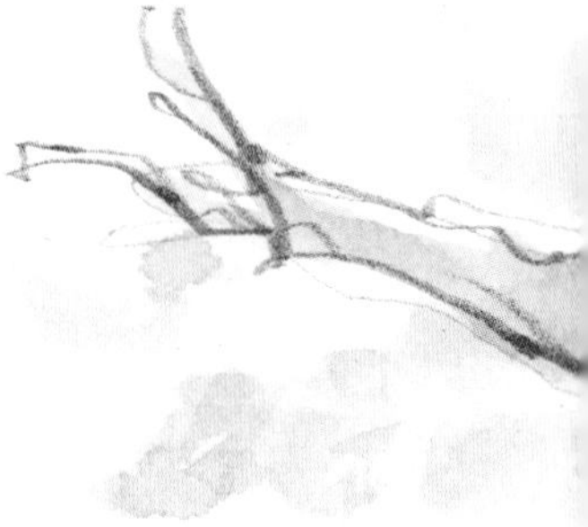

Gus thought about that.
His baseball cards
and plastic rattlesnake
and flashlight
were all solids.
But Gus didn't want
to show them again.

One day after school,
Gus's mother took him to play
at Grandpa's house.
"I need a solid,
a liquid, or a gas
to take for show-and-tell,"
Gus told Grandpa.

"You can take Skipper,"
Grandpa said.
"The more table scraps
I feed Skipper,
the more solid he gets."

Gus shook his head.
He didn't think Skipper
was the right kind of solid.

"Well, look around,"
Grandpa said.

Gus looked through Grandpa's house.
Gus looked through Grandpa's shed.
All Grandpa's things were old
and dusty and broken-down.
They weren't the right kind
of solids, either.

"How about a balloon?"
Grandpa suggested.
"If you blow it up,
it's a solid on the outside
and a gas on the inside."

Gus thought that
was a good idea.

Gus took a blown-up
balloon for show-and-tell.
Melissa had a balloon, too.
So did Alex,
and Emily,
and Lucas,
and Joe,
and Jenni.

Almost everyone else
had rocks.
Rocks were very boring,
but they were very solid.

Ryan Mason did a science experiment.
He made a gas
out of vinegar and baking soda.
It bubbled and blew up a balloon.
Mrs. Hall called the principal
and the custodian
to see Ryan's experiment.

Gus had to admit that
it was a great experiment.
He hated show-and-tell
more than ever.

Colorado History

"I need a show-and-tell
on Colorado history,"
Gus told his parents
the week after that.

"You could wear
your cowboy costume,"
Gus's mother said.
"There were a lot of cowboys
in Colorado history."

Gus made a face.
Costumes were for Halloween.
He would feel silly
being the only kid
wearing a costume
on a regular school day.

"What about your
piece of fool's gold?"
Gus's father said.
"A lot of people
came to Colorado
to find gold."

Gus looked for
the fool's gold,
but he couldn't find it.
Besides,
too many kids
had brought rocks
as their solids.
Gus was tired of rocks.

At Grandpa's house,
Gus looked
for a cool show-and-tell
on Colorado history.

"I've got nothing here
but Colorado history,"
Grandpa told Gus.
"I've lived seventy years
of Colorado history."

Grandpa found some pictures
of *his* grandpa and grandma
coming to Colorado
over a hundred years ago.
Grandpa's grandpa wore a beard.
Grandpa's grandma wore a bonnet.

Grandpa told Gus about the time
his grandpa had fallen
down a well.

He told Gus about the time
his grandma had shot a bear.

Gus loved looking at the pictures.
But he knew that Ryan Mason
would have more
for show-and-tell
than a bunch of crackly
old photographs.

Still, the pictures were better
than a cowboy costume or a rock,
especially a rock
that Gus couldn't even find.
If Gus took Grandpa's pictures
to show,
maybe he could remember
some of Grandpa's stories
to tell.
Maybe he could try
to tell them
the way Grandpa did.
Then Gus had
a wonderful idea.

The Best Show-and-Tell Ever

"All right, class,"
Mrs. Hall said
first thing on Friday morning.
"It's time for show-and-tell.
I know you have all brought
something interesting
on Colorado history
to share with the rest of us."

Melissa showed a book
from her summer vacation
at Mesa Verde.
Alex showed a cowboy hat
like Gus's cowboy hat
at home.
Gus scrunched down in his seat.
He wanted to be
the last to go.

Ryan Mason was waving his hand.
Ryan showed a model
of a covered wagon
that he had built from a kit.
He showed three Indian arrowheads.
He showed four flakes of gold
that he had panned himself.

"Oh, my," Mrs. Hall said.

Then Mrs. Hall turned
to look at Gus.
Gus's desk had
nothing on it.
"Did you forget
that we had show-and-tell
today, Gus?"
Mrs. Hall asked.

"No," Gus said.
"My show-and-tell is too big
to fit on my desk,
so I left it in the hall."

Gus went out into the hall.
He came back
with his show-and-tell.
His show-and-tell was Grandpa!

Mrs. Hall let Grandpa sit
in her rocking chair.
The children sat on the floor
in front of him.
Grandpa showed them
his long-ago pictures
and told them
his long-ago stories.

When he was done,
everybody clapped.

Ryan whispered to Gus,
"I wish my grandpas could come
for show-and-tell.
But they live too far away."

Even though Ryan always had
great show-and-tells,
Gus felt a little sorry
for him today.

Today Gus had
the best show-and-tell
that anyone could ever have.
He had Grandpa.